KU-586-747

THE SCHOOL IN MURKY WOOD

THE SCHOOL IN MURKY WOOD

Malcolm Bird

ORCHARD BOOKS

GRAMPIAN REGION
SCHOOLS LIBRARY SERVICE

For Annice Crossley

20034270

MORAY COUNCIL
LIBRARIES &
INFORMATION SERVICES
JA

ORCHARD BOOKS
96 Leonard Street, London EC2A 4RH
Orchard Books Australia
14 Mars Road, Lane Cove, NSW 2066
ISBN 1 85213 449 6 (hardback)
ISBN 1 85213 506 9 (paperback)
First published in Great Britain 1992
First paperback publication 1993
Text and illustrations © Malcolm Bird 1992

A CIP catalogue record for this book is available from the British Library.
Printed in Belgium

Darkness has fallen in Murky Wood. The children finished school hours ago. Now, it's time for the monsters to arrive for *their* lessons . . .

Miss Moist, the teacher, takes the register and calls out the names of the monsters in her class. Tonight all are present and correct.

Before lessons begin, the classroom pets must be looked after. Grisly shakes the bats awake while Dimpsey and Clammy fetch the fly jar – they'll be hungry!

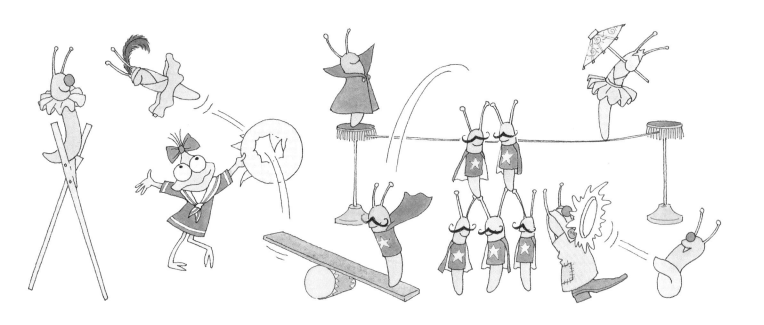

Squirmy is teaching the slugs some new tricks. The
spiders are escaping all over the place. Snarlene isn't
at all happy.

Lessons are fun at Murky Wood. The monsters in Miss Moist's class are eager to read stories, write lists of their favourite things, and count on their fingers and toes.

In home spoiling class, the monsters have to make a mess. They treat the classroom like someone's home.

They drop fluff and nail clippings on the floor,
put spiders in high places, stuff paper tissues into dirty
washing, hide socks, and put grimy rings around sinks.

Tonight Miss Moist and her class are trying out a new experiment. It starts out as rubbish and ends up as slime – the very best thing to rub into monsters' skin.

"Dinner time!" calls Miss Moist, ringing all the bells.
"Food at last!" shout her class.

The monsters make a dash for the canteen. They love the food that Mrs Wormold, the dinner lady, has made. It smells really disgusting.

Mr Brine, the headmaster, is a stickler for bad manners. Grunter is the best. He already has a gold star for greed.

It's howling practice next – the best lesson of all! Mr Brine urges them to be as noisy as they can.

The whole building shakes and shudders. The
monsters have never howled so loud before.

In art class Miss Moist poses gracefully while the monsters express themselves. They're all very artistic.

Next the monsters settle down to do their own special projects — like making spooky puppets or knitting a scarf to eat . . .

or constructing a robot Snarlene-catcher.

The last lesson is grumpy dancing. Miss Moist does a demonstration. She stamps her feet and kicks her toes, waves her arms and wrinkles her nose.

One, two, one, two – the monsters all join in:
stamping, frowning, scowling, snarling, with
grumpy faces for good grumpy dancing!

The sun is rising in Murky Wood. It's time for the monsters to go home. All their things must be taken down and hidden away.

Miss Moist checks that the classroom is exactly as
they found it, and the monsters start to leave.

Squirmy is the last to go. She almost gets discovered by the first arrival of the day.

So if you arrive at school one morning and everything isn't *quite* where it should be, keep your eyes open. There may be monsters using *your* school, too!